KU-636-969

THIS BOOK BELONGS TO

....

For Pierrette, who loves to dive into crazy and wonderful worlds!

First published in Great Britain 2021 by Egmont Books

An imprint of HarperCollins*Publishers*

1 London Bridge Street, London SE1 9GF

egmontbooks.co.uk

HarperCollinsPublishers

1st Floor, Watermarque Building, Ringsend Road Dublin 4, Ireland

Text copyright © 2021 Egmont Books UK Ltd

Interior illustrations by Dynamo © 2021 Egmont Books UK Ltd

Special thanks to Rachel Delahaye
Text design by Janene Spencer
With thanks to Speckled Pen for their help in the development of the series.

ISBN 978 07555 0126 7

Printed and bound in Great Britain by CPI Group

1

MIX
Paper from
responsible sources
FSC™ C007454

This book is produced from independently certified FSC™ paper
to ensure responsible forest management.

For more information visit: www.harpercollins.co.uk/green

SUPER CUTE

THE SLEEPOVER
SURPRISE

YOU ARE INVITED

PIP BIRD

EGMONT

THE WORLD OF SUPER CUTE

VANILLA VALLEY

THE BLOSSOM FESTIVAL

RITZY AVENUE

THE MARSHMALLOW CANYON

DEE'S HOME

MOMII

THE MUSEUM OF MOST IMPORTANT ITEMS

CONTENTS

CHAPTER ONE

An Inviting Day!

It was a dazzling day in the World of Cute. The bubblegum flowers had popped at dawn and their strawberry aroma filled the air. Swarms of glass-hoppers dipped in and out of the flower fields and their shiny little wings scattered sun rays far and wide. The spectacle woke everyone from Marshmallow Canyon to the Sandy Beaches. It even woke Sammy the sloth,

1

who usually snoozed until much later in the day.

Tickled awake by the sparkling light and delicious breeze, Sammy stood at the entrance to Snoozy Hollow, yawned and smiled at the sky.

It's a perfect day for . . . What was it, now? Sammy gave himself a very big wake-up shake . . . *It's a perfect day for writing my party invitations!*

'Thank goodness for the dazzling morning,' he sighed. 'Or I'd have slept most of the day and missed my dear friend, Louis. He should be here any minute. I must stretch!'

Sammy stepped out and began his sun salutation yoga routine. He reached high to the candyfloss clouds in the sky, then down to the daisies at his feet, which tried to tickle his toes.

Just as he was getting into a deep stretch, he heard a loud barking. It was nothing to do with his downward dog position – it was Louis. The labradoodle was running in circles round the meadow.

'Sammy! Sammy! Where are you?' Louis shouted.

Where am I? Sammy pondered. 'Well, in relation to the universe, I'm on a small planet called the World of Cute, but more specifically I am in the area known as the Dipsy Daisy Meadow. If you want to narrow it down further, you could say I was –'

'I can't see you!' Louis called.

Oops! Sammy had forgotten his camouflage coat was grass-green! He changed his fur to purple, one of his favourite colours. 'Can you see me now?' he asked.

As the labradoodle bounded towards him, Sammy quickly finished his yoga and reached behind to scratch his –

'Fleas, Sammy?' said Louis.

'No, no, no.' Sammy blushed. 'Just an itch on the . . . never mind. How lovely to see you, Louis. It's so kind of you to offer to help with the invitations. Did you bring all your pens and pencils?'

'All right here!' Louis said, tapping his magic nose.

Sammy had met Louis the labradoodle at the Blossom Festival, where he had been deftly doodling doodles. And not just deftly doodling doodles, but deftly doodling doodles *with his nose*! Louis had a very special nose, and he was a brilliant artist.

In fact, Sammy had met a *lot* of new friends at the Blossom Festival. That's why he was having a party. And he wanted the invitations to be extra special.

Louis was eager to get started. He pulled a pile of papers from his pocket. 'Shall we begin? What shall I do?'

'First let's decorate the paper,' Sammy suggested. 'Let's make every invitation beautiful, original, different, marvellous, unique . . .'

'You've got it!' Louis said.

The little dog scribbled furiously with his nose. Every time he needed a new colour he simply twitched his nose. Sammy watched with delight.

There were puffs of chalk and sprays of glitter as Louis added the finishing flourishes. Then he stood back, panting as if he'd run a marathon.

Sammy looked down at the beautiful papers laid out on the grass. There were summer scenes, magic whirlwinds, melted colours and

dripping rainbows. Each one was a masterpiece. The dipsy daisies began to toss them in the air to dry the ink.

'Wait, dipsies!' said Sammy. 'We haven't done the words yet. Are you ready, Louis?'

Louis twitched his nose and Sammy told him what to write.

You Are Invited to
Sammy's Sleepover!
Wear your favourite onesie and
bring your favourite toy.
Time: 5pm, this Saturday

'Okay, dipsies, do your thing!' Sammy said, and the daisies tossed the invitations in the air to dry them. They landed back on the grass in a neat pile.

'Bravo!' Sammy cried. 'Let's post them right now.'

'You've forgotten something,' Louis said. 'I haven't written *where the party is*.'

Sammy's eyes shone with mischief. 'Oh!' he said. 'Well, it's a surprise.'

'But we all need to meet *somewhere*,' said Louis.

Sammy chuckled. 'Just put: *Meet at the Wish Tree*. We can walk to the party location from there. No one will ever guess where we're going!'

The extra detail was added to each invitation. Then Louis and Sammy tucked them into golden envelopes and set off to the post box. Louis ran ahead, but returned, his ears flattened with worry.

'The humpygrump hummingbird is nesting in the post box again!' he said. 'I've just seen her pelt Kevin the kettle with poo!'

'Humpygrump poo is the prettiest poo in the World of Cute,' Sammy said. He knew so many facts! 'It has more colours than a rainbow! But also more bad smells than a stinky bog competition. We'll just have to deliver the invitations ourselves. It's a shame I can't walk faster.'

Skye the skateboard trundled to a stop in front of Sammy and Louis.

'Hey, hop on!' she said. 'I'll take you anywhere you want to go. I've got a bit of free time and four wheels that need exercising!'

As usual in the World of Cute, there was always a perfect solution!

'Cornucopia Avenue, please, Skye!' Sammy said.

As they scooted along, Sammy was greeted by lots of friends. Everyone was surprised to see him out of bed so early.

'Morning, Sammy!' called Tina the toaster.

'Breakfast on the go?' She popped out some ready-buttered slices. They smelled so delicious that Sammy and Louis snatched them up and gobbled them down.

'Hi, Sammy. It's a bit early for you!' giggled Fleur the robot fox. She was taking her mechanical cubs for a walk. Sammy turned his fur pink to make the cubs laugh. Their giggles made a pretty tinkling sound, like wind chimes. The World of Cute seemed particularly cute today!

In Cornucopia Avenue, Sammy and Louis had no trouble finding Lucky the lunacorn's house. It was a pretty stable made with twisting tree trunks and woven with flowers, and on the ground right outside was a pile of sparkling confetti.

'Glittery mess is a side effect of having a magical horn,' Sammy said. 'When the moon comes out, Lucky's horn just glows. But when friendship is about, there's no knowing what it'll do!'

Sammy rang the silvery doorbell and waited. He peered in the window.

'What can you see?' Louis asked.

'There's a display of rosettes on the back wall, strawberry hay baskets in the corners of the room and a large vase of glorious sunflowers on the table. Ah!' Sammy turned bright yellow as he remembered the first time he and Lucky

13

met, in the middle of a sunflower field on a glorious summer's day. She was on her way to enter the Cuteness Competition at the Blossom Festival. Little did Sammy know at the time, but he was about to meet the best friends in the world!

'Can you see any lunacorns?' Louis said, leaping to look.

'I don't think there's anyone home,' said Sammy. 'Oh dear. I don't want to leave the invitation at the door in case it blows away. We'll have to come back later. Next stop, Blueberry Hill.'

CHAPTER 2

Oh, Flip!

With the help of Skye the skateboard, Sammy and Louis got to Blueberry Hill in no time. Or *snow* time!

'Wh-wh-what's going on?' Sammy stuttered.

The hill was famous for its purple grasses, but now it was dazzling white. At the top, Sammy and Louis could see a little figure, sliding down the hill very fast.

'Is that Pip the pineapple?' Louis asked.

'Yes! I think you're right,' Sammy said. 'And that's Cami the cloud right above her.' He touched the snow with his fingers. 'Cami made snow so Pip can ski *and* keep cool!'

'That tropi-*cool* fruit pineapple sure likes to chill,' said Louis.

Sammy squinted hard at the mountain top. His heart flipped at the sight of his friends, and he hollered as loudly as he could: 'Yoo-hoo! Party invitations!'

Cami and Pip looked confused.

'Can you hear Sammy, Pip?' said Cami.

'Um, yes?' said Pip. 'But I can't see him anywhere!'

Louis gave Sammy a nudge. 'Your coat!' he said.

Sammy had a serious word with himself about camouflaging at awkward times. Then he turned his fur from snow-white to orange.

'It *is* you, Sammy!' Pip called, launching into an excited downhill triple-flip. The acrobatic pineapple never missed a chance to do something gymnastic and seeing a friend was the best excuse ever. Only, Pip lost her concentration and her triple-flip turned into a single flip, followed by a flump and a roly-poly all the way down to the bottom of the hill.

'I guess that's the end of my al*pine*-apple skiing session!' Pip laughed as she leaped up and dusted herself down. 'What's up, Sammy?'

'I've just come to deliver these.' Sammy handed out the invitations.

Cami and Pip read them quickly. Pip did a handstand for joy and Cami squealed with excitement.

'A sleepover party?' Cami cried. 'I'm on

cloud nine. Wait, I AM cloud nine!'

After giving Sammy and Louis lots of big hugs, Pip and Cami went on their way, singing *Onesie World, here we come!*

Next on Sammy's list was Dee the dumpling kitty. She lived on the other side of Blueberry Hill. Skye the skateboard had things to do, but Sammy and Louis were happy to walk and watch the World of Cute embrace the day.

They laughed at the rows of fancy ants setting off for work, doing the can-can in formation. They stuck out their tongues as the flying frying-pans overhead spilled sizzling sherbet. The tangy breeze that blew in from the Fruit Salad Forests filled them with zest. It felt as if everything was excited for Sammy's party.

When they reached Dee's street, Sammy couldn't see the dumpling kitty's bamboo palace anywhere. In fact, there was nothing but a strange black tent!

'Oh dear. Perhaps Dee has moved house?' Sammy said.

A voice came from inside the tent. 'No! I still live here!'

Dee emerged, polishing off some breakfast cake. Her little pink tongue flicked around her face, collecting crumbs and giving her fur a good wash at the same time.

'Yesterday, I made a three-storey house out of origami paper,' she said. 'Then, in the middle of the night, the rainbow rain poured right through and I had to make something else. I didn't plan to make a tent out of liquorice, but I was half asleep at the time.'

'Liquorice!' Louis crept closer and gave Dee's house a quick lick. 'Yum!'

Sammy shook his head at his own forgetfulness. 'Of course!' he said. 'Silly me. Why would you always live in the same house when you can make a different one every day with your cute craft kit?'

'That's right,' said Dee. 'I'm always *itching* to make something new. Is that why you're itching too, Sammy?'

Sammy blushed. 'I didn't even know I was!' he said.

'I'm amazed you haven't made yourself a cake castle,' said Louis.

Dee looked surprised. 'I did. But I ate it.'

'Could you make one out of crayons for me?' asked the labradoodle.

'Of course,' said the dumpling kitty. 'I've built knitted nooks for woolly monkeys and lollipop lairs for licky lions. I can make anything you like!'

'Are you any good at making onesies?' Sammy asked with a little smile.

He handed Dee the invitation. When she read it, her fur fluffed up with excitement.

'Oh yes!' she cried. 'Thank you, Sammy. I'll make one right away.'

'Before you do . . . Lucky the lunacorn isn't home.' Sammy tapped the golden envelope containing Lucky's invite. 'In case we don't catch her, could you tell her all about the party and where to be?'

'Certainly!' Dee grinned. 'I'll even make her a onesie. Sammy?' She looked around. *'Sammy?'*

'What are you doing?' Louis barked at Sammy, who was climbing a nearby tree.

'Just checking out the napping spots,' Sammy called. 'In case I . . . ZZZZZZ.'

All the fast talking had exhausted the sloth, who had got out of bed way too early. He was now fast asleep in a cradle of branches.

'What shall we do?' Louis asked. 'Wake him up?'

'Sloths just don't have the same kind of energy as cats and dogs,' said Dee. 'Let him sleep for a little bit.'

The dumpling kitty plucked knitting needles from her fur and quickly crocheted a blanket. Then she and Louis threw it up and over the branch where Sammy was snoofling and dreaming of fascinating facts. Louis doodled a note and left it underneath the tree: *See you at the party, Sammy!*

'I need to get started on the onesies,' Dee said. 'What about you, Louis?'

'I'm going home to work on my painting,' said Louis. 'It's called *The A-Z of Cute*. I'm drawing the whole World of Cute in one picture, from the apple usherettes to the zippy zebras with detachable stripes.'

'Sounds great, Louis,' Dee said. 'And it

gives me a great idea for a onesie! See you at the party!'

With everyone busying – or snoozing – nobody saw the golden envelope containing Lucky's invitation slip from sleeping Sammy's paw. It floated down on the breeze like a sycamore seed. Then it was caught by the wind and swirled up and up, like a kite. Over the broccoli trees and the milky clouds it went,

travelling across town before skittering along Ritzy Avenue, where a little dog was taking a siesta on his porch. The flutter made him open one round eye.

A golden letter . . . It *must* be an invitation! He sprang to his little legs.

'Glamour Gang, fetch!' he yipped.

The dog's obedient friends – a pizza slice, a snail, a muffin and a scooter – rushed to bring him the envelope. His paws shook with excitement as he carefully opened the envelope and pulled out the paper, decorated with confetti and spiralled horns. A party! A secret sleepover! With onesies!

He clutched it to his chest, trembling from

the tops of his ears to the tips of his tiny tail. His whiskers shivered and his tutu quivered as he imagined his theatrical entrance, wearing the best onesie in the world. It was going to be a party no one would ever forget.

And with Clive the chihuahua, that was probably true . . .

CHAPTER 3

Fizzy Fun

It was five o'clock on Saturday and Sammy was standing beneath the Wish Tree, wearing a snappy-toothed shark onesie. Worried that he might fall asleep waiting for his friends, he said all the facts he knew about the Wish Tree out loud to keep him alert. Talking also made the shark teeth on his onesie SNAP, which was fun.

'The Wish Tree is at least five thousand years old and only grants kind wishes,' Sammy said to himself. 'It doesn't make *all* wishes come true, so it's a good idea to hug the tree tight and wish the wish with all your might.'

What a good idea! Sammy hugged the Wish Tree tightly and wished with all his might that everyone would have a wonderful time at his party and enjoy all of the surprises he had in store! Under his onesie, his camouflaging fur turned brown to match the Wish Tree trunk.

When Pip turned up, she jumped with shock!

'There's a shark hugging the Wish Tree!' she cried, leaping into the branches for safety.

'It's only me!' Sammy said. 'It's my onesie! See?' He let go of the trunk and made his fur turn yellow so Pip could see his face and paws.

'Oh Sammy, that's brilliant!' Pip said. 'Although perhaps you should try not to camouflage, in case we pass anyone who's easily spooked, like the scaredy-cat cactus or the elephantimouse.'

'Good idea, Pip,' Sammy said. 'Let's see your onesie.'

Pip jumped down from the Wish Tree branches and twirled like they did on the catwalks at Cutie Fashion Week. Her onesie had short coffee-coloured fur and a hood with a little black nose.

'You're a pug, Pip!' Sammy declared. 'A pineapple pug!'

'A *sporty* pineapple pug,' Pip corrected. She cartwheeled around the Wish Tree to make her point.

A cloud passed overhead, casting a cool shade. Pip sighed with relief. 'That's better,' she said. 'I was feeling hot after all that cartwheeling.'

Sammy looked up, feeling worried. It wasn't going to rain on the party day, was it?

'Cami!' Sammy cried with delight.

Cami was wearing a cow onesie, complete with dangling legs and a swishing tail.

'I'm a MOO-ving cloud!' Cami giggled.

Sammy's heart was filling up fast with happiness. Everyone was putting lots of effort into dressing up for the sleepover, just as he'd hoped.

'I spy a zebra,' Cami said from her lookout

spot above the tree. 'A zebra with a horn? That's strange.'

Lucky trotted towards her friends. 'Sorry I'm late. I've been giving rides at a funny bunny birthday party all afternoon! Dee told me all about the sleepover. So exciting! This zebricorn is ready to party!' She gave a twirl. 'Look, I've got zip-up detachable stripes!'

Sammy, Cami and Pip clapped. 'You look amazing,' Pip said.

'It's all thanks to Dee the dumpling kitty,' said Lucky. 'She made it for me. Say hi, Dee!'

Dee was tucked behind the wings on Lucky's back. She popped out and waved. 'It's me, Dee the dee-licious ice-lolly!' She wore a frosty pink onesie covered in sprinkles. A few dropped off every time she moved. 'Oops,' she said. 'I think I used milk instead of glue.'

'RAARGGH—RUFF!' Louis the labradoodle suddenly appeared in a dragon onesie. He tried his roar again. 'RRRRAAAAR! I'm a labradoodledragon!'

Pip giggled. 'You're a mouthful, more like!'

'Louis, that's a remarkable costume,' Lucky said. 'Paws with roars!'

'Who else are we waiting for?' Sammy asked, rubbing his hands together.

They looked around. Lucky, Louis, Cami, Pip, Dee and Sammy. They were all there, weren't they?

'We're waiting for NO-ONESIE!' Sammy chuckled. 'Let's go!'

'Where are we going?' Cami said, swinging her cow legs and bopping Pip on the head.

Sammy paused for effect. He enjoyed the anticipation.

Lucky drummed her hooves impatiently.

'Tell us, tell us!' she cried.

'We're going to MOMII!' Sammy cheered.

There was silence.

'The . . . Museum of Most Important Items?' Lucky asked.

'The museum no one ever goes to because it's so boring?' Pip said.

'Last time I went there, I had to pinch my whiskers to stay awake,' Dee said.

'Maybe that's how Sammy stays awake,' Pip said with a giggle. 'By pinching his . . .'

Pip trailed off when she saw Lucky shake her head and point to Sammy. The sloth was looking down in the mouth behind his snappy shark teeth.

'Do you know what I think?' Lucky said in a jolly voice. 'I think that a sleepover party with very best friends is the very best place to be, no matter where it is. Who agrees?'

All the super cutes cheered and patted Sammy until the smile returned to his face. Then they formed a conga line – a wonderful row of roaring, sparkling, stripy, snappy, pug-a-licious partygoers – and they danced and kicked their way into the town centre.

Cuties lined the street to watch them. Toffee apples teetered on their sticks to get a good view. Funny bunnies jumped high in the air so they could see the fabulous onesies. Even Hannah the hairbrush, who usually liked to be

centre of attention, brushed Lucky's mane as the lunacorn swished past.

The friends conga-danced from the Fanfare Gardens through Marshmallow Canyon. When

they arrived at Mane Street, the air was thick
with the smell of bubblegum flowers, making
their tummies rumble. Sammy stopped the
conga line.

'Who wants a refreshment stop at the Pink Lemonade Hot Tub?' he cried.

'We all do!' his friends replied. They ran to the hot tub, where they dipped paper cups into the pool of lemonade. Cami scooped up handfuls of infusing strawberries and scattered them in all the cups. Then they all counted,

'ONE ... TWO ... THREE!'

The lemonade turned pink. Strawberry-shaped sparkles exploded and popped in the air above everybody, with bursts of delicious fruit scent.

'I love pink lemonade,' Cami sighed. She sucked it up through a straw and her cloud fluff blushed the colour of strawberries.

'It hits the spot,' said Pip. **'AAAAAAH!'**

It hit Louis's spot a little too hard. The little dog began to leap about like a labradoodledragon in a pinball machine.

'If you have any more, you'll take off like a proper dragon!' Dee giggled.

The jokes were flowing and the lemonade was disappearing and the super cutes were doing what super cutes loved to do – have fun with friends. Nothing could possibly go wrong.

But following from a safe distance, sneaking through the bristle-pad bushes, was an unexpected guest. A guest just waiting for the right moment to trot into the party and shake things up . . .

CHAPTER 4

It Had to be Poo

After a journey full of bubbles and giggles, the super cutes arrived at the grand-looking Museum of Most Important Items. To their surprise, the window shutters were shut and the front door firmly locked.

Cami hovered above the door. 'Oh dear, maybe we can't get in. Maybe we'll have to have the party somewhere else,' she said hopefully.

'Or maybe we can just do the sleepover another time,' Pip suggested in a trembly voice.

'Your eyes are worried, Pip,' said Lucky gently. 'Is this your first ever sleepover?'

Pip nodded.

'There's no need to worry,' said Lucky. 'We'll all look after you. Won't we, everyone?'

'We'll take good care of you,' said Sammy.

'Whenever you feel nervous, we're here for a cuddle!' Cami said, cocooning Pip in her cloud fluff.

'Good evening.' A little pig wearing a dark green MOMII uniform and wellies appeared at side of the building. He fixed his hat firmly on his head. 'Super cutes? This way, if you wouldn't mind.' He beckoned with his trotter.

'He's adorable!' whispered Lucky as the cutes followed the very professional micropig to a side entrance.

'So cute!' Pip agreed.

'SHHHH!' said the pig. He whipped a piece of paper from his top pocket. 'If you're not on the list, you're not coming in.'

'Before we tell you our names, could you tell us yours?' Cami said, sweetly.

The little pig took off his hat and clutched it. 'I'm Micky the mini-pig. BUT I'LL BE A BIG PIG SOON!'

'Totally adorable,' Lucky sighed.

'My seven brothers and sisters are all bigger than me now,' Micky said more softly. 'But it's only because I'm the youngest. I'll grow.'

'Of course you will,' Sammy said, resisting the urge to pat the piggy on the head. 'And I can confirm that all these cutes here are on the list. No need to check, Micky.'

Micky ticked off their names anyway, just to make it official, then he folded the paper neatly back in his pocket. 'Follow me.'

They entered the museum side door and followed Micky down a little corridor to the main lobby. Huge gold pillars towered from floor to ceiling. It didn't look this big from the outside.

'WOOOOOOW!' Pip gasped, staring. 'That roof is very high!'

Cami floated up to take a look, but suddenly . . .

SCREEEEECH!

The noise made Cami shrivel in fear and shoot back down to her friends.

'That's just Olive the night-shift security owl,' Micky explained. 'She's here to make sure you don't touch anything.'

'DON'T TOUCH ANYTHING!' Olive screeched. She glided into the next room like a giant leaf carried on the wind.

Sammy thought he knew the museum inside out. But he'd never been at night, so he'd never met Olive before. He knew owls were wise, but he didn't realise they were so strict!

I hope this doesn't scare my friends and ruin everything, he thought. Perhaps the Wish Tree had chosen not to help him.

Dee saw Sammy looking sad. She clapped her paws. 'Do you know what? This is the COOLEST place for a sleepover,' she said. 'Before we snore, let's explore! Sammy, why don't you show us your favourite items in the museum?' She looked at Lucky.

'Yes!' said Lucky at once. 'We would LOVE to know all about the fascinating things here. It's like a treasure trove of . . .' She nudged Pip with her horn.

'. . . of things that will blow our minds!' Pip said, doing a leap and prickling Cami's fluff.

'I bet there are things we didn't even know existed!' Cami said.

'And I can't wait to draw it all when I get back home!' Louis said excitedly.

Sammy peered through his snappy-shark onesie teeth. He opened his mouth wide as if he was about to yawn . . . but words came tumbling out instead.

'Well, first let me show you a collection of wooden rulers,' he said happily. 'They come in inches and centipede-i-metres, because they used to measure things in insects! And you're really going to want to see the tremendous collection of poo.'

'So *that's* why you know so much about poo,' Louis said, wrinkling his nose.

'Poo is fascinating,' Sammy said. 'And these specimens have been preserved brilliantly! Now, here's a choco-spread jar poo. Rather surprisingly, it's green! And this pile of poo comes from twirling tea-cups. They're sugar-cube plops!'

Lucky managed an impressed whistle.

Dee giggled. 'Instead of spooky stories at our sleepover, we can tell poopy stories!'

'**SHHH!**' said Micky the museum pig. 'Quiet in the museum, please! You must obey the museum rules!'

The friends walked in silence through hall after hall of glass cabinets and shelves, filled with tiny pieces of cute history. They were all secretly wondering when the sleepover fun was going to happen.

Outside, the day turned into evening. The sun sank low and the old building was plunged into grey dusky light. Everyone ducked as Olive the owl swooped low over their heads.

'Isn't this the best place for a sleepover party!' Sammy said enthusiastically.

'How did you get us into a museum at night, Sammy?' Lucky whispered.

Sammy grinned. 'Well, I give so much of my time to the museum, researching facts about the exhibits, that they were happy to let me have a party here.'

Louis sneezed.

'SHHH, Mr Labradoodle please!' said Micky.

'They don't look very happy to me,' Pip said.

'Pip, you have to be more thoughtful or it'll upset Sammy,' Lucky whispered so that Sammy couldn't hear.

'I know. It's just a pity it's not more . . .

exciting,' Pip squeaked.

Micky's piggy face fell. He shuffled closer. 'Do you think this place is boring?' he said anxiously. 'Over the years, everyone has lost interest in the museum. Now, nobody comes at all, unless they're lost and looking for directions.'

'Oh Micky, that's so sad,' Cami said, hovering comfortingly above the mini-pig. 'You must be very lonely here without visitors to look after.'

Micky shrugged. 'Well, it's a nice place to work if you're trying to escape the squealing racket at home,' he said. 'Besides, this job trots in the family. My father worked here as museum guard before me. And my father's father. And my father's father's father. And before that it was a burger named Bob. But that's not important.'

Louis tapped his nose. 'Shall I write that down?'

There was no time. Micky was letting it all out. 'It was never meant to be a boring place,' he wailed. 'It was built to house the magnificent history of the World of Cute. It was supposed to inspire everyone. Now it inspires nobody at all.'

'It inspires Sammy,' Cami said.

Micky the mini-pig sighed. 'That's the trouble. It *only* inspires Sammy. If something doesn't happen to make more people visit the museum, it'll have to close for good.'

BONG! BONG! BONG!

'What was that?' Cami gasped.

Micky checked his pocket watch. 'Just the museum bell. It's seven o'clock.'

'Seven o'clock already?' Sammy said, rushing over from an ancient crafting exhibit that he'd been showing to Dee. 'Then, my friends, it's time that we visited the Museum Café. We can't go to bed before we are fed!'

CHAPTER 5

Pickles Versus Prickles

'Yay! I'm in the mood for food!' Louis barked.

The cutes chatted and giggled their way down the corridors to the Museum Café. This part of the building was modern and shiny.

'Wait here!' said Sammy at the door. He scuttled into the café and fetched dinner from the kitchen area. Then he placed it on to the table, ready to eat.

'Come in!' he called.

When the cutes entered, they couldn't believe their eyes! The side wall of the café was made of glass, and it looked out on to the Twinkle Pastures, where glow-bugs flickered like candles. There was a long table down the middle of the room with plates and napkins, jugs of colour-changing juices and tealights. And there was an enormous bowl of steaming spaghetti in tomato sauce, with baskets of doughballs and dips.

'Ta-da!' Sammy said. 'A tummy-warming feast!'

The whole scene was so magical and the smells so good! The cutes gathered round

Sammy and gave him a big hug.

'This is beautiful, Sammy!' Lucky gasped.

'If you think this is pretty, look up,' Sammy said with a big smile.

'*Whoooa!*' everyone cried. The ceiling was made of glass, too, and they could see the stars popping out of the dark sky like sequins.

'You can see the constellations,' Sammy said. 'There's the Celestial Mint Chew, and the Starry Bucket . . .'

Louis whipped out an easel and started doodling the pretty star patterns.

High above them all, the moon crossed the sky. White-blue moonlight shone through the glass ceiling . . .

Micky snorted in surprise. 'What's happening to the unicorn?' he squeaked.

The moonlight had fallen on Lucky's face, and her magical horn was glowing like an ice fire.

Pip giggled. 'She's a *lunacorn*, Micky! Her

horn shines in the moonlight. Nothing to be scared of.'

'I'm not scared,' Micky said. 'Only little pigs get scared and I'm NOT LITTLE.'

TAP TAP TAP.

'What's that?' said Cami.

TAP TAP TAP.

The cutes looked up.

'Why is there a cactus in a tutu sitting on top of the glass roof?' said Dee with a puzzled frown.

The top section of the cactus flipped back to reveal . . . the face of a little dog with beady eyes and twitchy whiskers.

'*CLIVE!*' everyone exclaimed.

Clive the chihuahua was on the roof!

'Did you invite Clive?' Pip asked Sammy in surprise.

Sammy shook his head.

Clive pushed a golden invitation envelope against the glass and tapped again.

'That's *Lucky's* invitation!' Sammy gasped. 'So *that's* where it went!'

'*Yoohooo*,' yapped a little voice. 'I've got an invitation. Let me in!'

The last time the super cutes had met Clive was at the Cuteness Competition at the Blossom Festival. The competitive little chihuahua had done nothing but yap and bully and stick his tutu where it wasn't welcome. He wasn't welcome now, either!

But it looked as if the cutes didn't have a choice. Clive had found an open window and was already squishing himself through. He clung to the window frame with his sharp claws. His cactus bottom wiggled dangerously high above the Museum Café.

'Catch me!' Clive squealed. 'NOW!'

Lucky quickly flew up to the glass roof – and caught Clive on her back. He was a bit ouchy

because of the cactus spikes on his onesie –
although Lucky was used to being spiked
by Pip.

Clive paraded up and down Lucky's back,
looking victorious. 'Now I'm here the party can
truly begin!' he yapped.

But Clive hadn't met Micky the mini-pig
museum guard yet.

Micky checked the piece of paper in his
pocket. 'Who are you?' the mini-pig said.
'Museum rules say that NO ONE can come into
the museum from the roof.'

'I'm Clive!' Clive said with a little shimmy of
his shoulders and a toss of his head. 'Everyone
knows me.'

'Well, I don't,' said Micky. 'And I'm in charge. This is a private sleepover party. There's nothing on the list about a Clive, a chihuahua or a cactus.'

Clive fluffed his tutu and stuck his pointy nose right into Micky's face. 'I've got an invitation,' he yipped. 'Anyway, I'm related to Clawdius Yapperton.'

Micky gasped. 'You mean the founder of the museum?' He pointed with a trembling trotter to a portrait on the café wall of a little dog with a velvet hat and Tudor ruff. Beneath it was a plaque:

Clawdius Yapperton 1525-1537

The best pedigree ever

Clawdius Yapperton 1525-1537
The best pedigree ever

Clive struck the same pose as the portrait. The haughty eyes, the tweaky nose, the confident eyebrow . . . There could be no mistake.

'As a descendant of the Yappertons, I have a lifetime pass to the museum and I can enter any time I like and no one can stop me,' squealed Clive. 'Isn't that right, Mucky?'

'It's Micky,' the little pig sniffed. 'And I suppose that the answer is yes.'

Clive jumped from Lucky's back to the ground. He bumped into Cami on the way down – 'OUCH' – and then Pip – 'OUCH' – and then Dee – 'OUCH!' The prickles from his cactus costume were so sharp that they went right through the super cutes' onesies.

'I would have come earlier,' Clive said. 'But I had a terrible time getting my tutu on over my onesie. I tore right through two skirts. I had to wake up Sally the sewing machine to demand that she make me another. By the time she'd got it exactly how I wanted, I'd missed the meeting at the Wish Tree.'

'Shame that's all you missed,' muttered Pip, pulling cactus spikes from Cami's cloud fluff.

'But I followed your trail and ... Ta-da! Here I am!' Clive did a twirl and managed to spike everyone again.

'What trail?' Sammy asked.

'OOOPS.' Dee the dumpling kitty blushed and pointed at her onesie. It was now a frosty pink ice-lolly with very few sprinkles left on it. 'He must have followed my sprinkles.'

'Isn't it lucky that the kitty isn't good at making onesies, or I wouldn't be here!' Clive said haughtily.

'Very lucky,' the others murmured, apart from Louis, who growled, and Dee, who rolled under the table to stop herself saying something rude.

'The happy mood around here is deflating quicker than a hedgehog's beachball,' said Lucky. She stamped her hoof. 'You know what I say about sleepover parties? The more sleeping bags, the merrier!'

Sammy gave her a grateful smile. Lucky was an amazi-corn! 'Let's have a big cheer now that everyone's here at the Secret Sleepover Party,' he said. 'Hip, hip . . .'

'Hooray!' cheered everyone.

'Yip!' cheered Clive.

They sat round the table and ladled delicious spaghetti on to their plates. They laughed as they sucked up the strands with slurpy noises and flicks of spaghetti sauce. As they crunched into their doughballs, they shared stories of how they'd chosen their onesies.

'I knew everyone would be cuddly and soft and *I* wanted to be original,' Clive said pompously. 'That's why I came as something spiky.'

'Sammy's onesie has spiky teeth,' Louis pointed out.

'And I AM spiky,' Pip said. 'All over!'

'What are you supposed to be?' Clive asked, prodding Pip's hood. 'A bug?'

'No, a PUG,' Pip growled. 'A Particularly Prickly Pug.'

'**SHHHH!**' Micky said. 'Remember the museum rules. Anyway, I think you *all* look marvellous.' He looked down at his wellies and sniffed.

'Oh!' said Dee. 'You don't have a onesie, Micky! You're still in your uniform!'

She dug around in her furry pockets and whipped out some knitting needles. With her instant crafting skills, the dumpling kitty made Micky a onesie in ten seconds flat. It was green and covered with lumps and bumps.

'What is it, what is it?' Micky squealed with excitement as he wriggled into the creation. He stood back and did a twirl.

'A pig in a pickle!' everyone cried in delight.

'Huh,' said Clive. 'That's not original OR glamorous.'

'Because nothing could be more glamorous than a cactus in a tutu?' Cami said crossly, turning a darker shade of grey.

When everyone had finished their dinner, Sammy called for attention. 'Are we fed and ready for bed?' he said.

'Yes!' cried the super cutes.

'Then the time has come to show you where you'll be sleeping!'

'Hurrah!' cried the friends.

'Just follow the trail!' Sammy pointed to a door on the other side of the café.

Filled with excitement, the members of the super cute sleepover club ran through the door. The museum was now in darkness, apart from a string of fairy lights on the floor. The friends tiptoed along the lights, all giggling with anticipation – apart from Pip, who made wobbly noises.

'It's a bit different to going to bed at home,' she said with a sniff.

'Don't be a baby – ow ... OW!' Clive stared

with bemusement at his bottom, where he'd felt several sharp nips.

Whenever someone upset her friends, Lucky's horn tingled. This time, it had released snappy snap-dragons to teach Clive a lesson!

'It's okay, Pip,' Cami said, cuddling the quivering pineapple. 'We're all right here.'

'Let's all hold hands, or hooves, trotters, tails or paws,' Lucky suggested.

76

They formed a chain and followed the lights that sparkled on the floor like fallen stars. The magical trail led them through big rooms, small rooms, corridors and passages. It eventually ended at a solid oak door.

'I want to be the first to see,' said Clive, striding to the front.

Pip flipped with excitement. Before he could put his paw on the handle, Clive was smooshed to the floor by the tumbling pineapple.

'My tutu!' Clive cried.

Pip had also knocked over Micky on her way down.

'My pickle has prickles,' Micky tutted, wriggling out from under Clive's cactus onesie.

'And my prickles have prickles!' Pip wailed.

The rest of the cutes laughed as Clive, Micky and Pip unwound themselves from their tongue-twisting tangle.

'Well, I'm *prickling* with excitement,' Lucky said. 'Let's all open the door together. ONE, TWO . . .'

But before Lucky could say THREE, Louis's waggy tail knocked the door handle – and it swung open all by itself.

CHAPTER 6

Making Magic Moments

The friends saw a thousand tiny glimmers, as if an overnight frost had settled everywhere. Swarms of glow-bugs were on the walls and ceiling of the museum, their little bodies blinking soft shades of white and yellow. Sheets had been stretched across the room to create tent canopies. Beneath the sheets, the floor was padded with cushions and pillows and sleeping bags, all softer than marshmallows and lit with lanterns.

The super cutes were so stunned they couldn't speak.

'Do you like it?' Sammy asked, nervously.

'We love it!' they whispered.

Cami floated upwards, collecting glow-bugs in her fluff. 'Look, I'm a cloud of sparkles!' she cried. Then she dropped the glow-bugs on top of the canopies, where their lights glowed softly on to the beds below.

'It'll be like sleeping under the stars,' Lucky said.

Louis bounded towards the cushions. The

other dog at the party marched round the room inspecting the situation.

'That cushion is mine,' Clive said, pointing at a red velvet one. 'And I want to sit there. No, *there*!'

'Go ahead, Clive,' Lucky said patiently. 'Once you're settled, we can all snuggle up and let the sleepover begin.'

Clive stood on his preferred cushion, turning in circles until he found the perfect position. The rest of the cutes nestled into the remaining spaces. Cami made sure she was beside Pip, in case the pineapple got scared.

'Thanks, Cami,' said Pip gratefully. 'I feel as snug as a pug in a rug!'

'This hog is going to sleep like a log,' Micky said.

Sammy produced a pack of cards. 'I thought we could play a game,' he said.

'How about Snap!?' Louis suggested, laughing as he pointed at Sammy's shark teeth.

By the light of the lanterns, the cutes played Snap! Clive painted his toenails and did a complicated bedtime beauty routine including lots of different creams and lotions. Slowly, the glow-bugs and lanterns began to fall asleep, turning off their little lights one by one until the tent was like a warm and glowing cave in the darkness.

'Let's pretend we're in a tent in the middle of the desert,' Cami said.

'Or in the middle of the ocean,' Lucky said.

'Let's imagine we're on a space shuttle drifting in space,' Dee said.

There was a little whimper. It was the sound of a chihuahua with the collywobbles. Cami drifted closer to Clive and cuddled him with her cloud fluff.

'I'm fine,' Clive said, pushing her away.

'Being scared is nothing to be ashamed of,' said Sammy.

'That gives me an idea,' Micky said, getting to his feet.

'Where's *Mucky* going?' Clive yapped, as the little pig trotted off into the darkness. But no one knew.

While Micky was away, the super cutes chatted and told stories. Then . . .

'Attention please!'

'Mucky's back!' Clive said. 'Have you bought something to soothe me?'

'It's Micky,' Micky said. 'And I have brought something for *everyone*. To take your mind off sleeping in a strange place, I've arranged a Sleepover Spectacle. You're about to meet a museum treasure that even Sammy has never seen.'

Sammy gasped. The other cutes weren't so impressed.

'More old stuff?' Pip sighed.

'**SHHHH!**' Micky said. 'Listen.'

There was a fluttering and clinking and thumping above the canopy.

'Wh-wh-what's that?' Pip said. 'I'm scared of things that go bump in the night.'

'Come and see,' said Micky with a smile.

The super cutes crept out from under the canopy. Through the sliver of moonlight in the top window, they could see funny-shaped rocks flapping, zooming and spinning around.

'What are they?' Dee said.

'They're fossils,' Micky said. He handed
out torches, one for each cute.

'M-m-moving fossils?' Pip said
shakily as she switched on her torch.

'**WHOA!**' This was an unusually loud
exclamation for Cami, who had floated up and
caught a fossil in the beam of her torch. 'I just
saw a flying milkshake!'

'These magic torches shine a light on what

our fossils used to be,'
Micky said. 'And we
all know that the
World of Cute is

full of the most extraordinary things. See for yourselves!'

The other super cutes turned on their torches and chased the fossils with their beams . . .

'Oh!' Sammy said, startled. 'I can see an ancient bubble-blower!'

'I've just caught a jumping bean!' Cami cried.

'Wow, look at this!' Lucky gasped. Dancing in her torchlight was the fossil of an octocat, its eight tails flicking and swishing.

'Now this is what I call FUN!' Pip said, forgetting her fear and somersaulting in the air.

'What do you think, Sammy?' Louis said. '*Sammy?*'

Sammy had fallen asleep on the floor. His

friends' whoops and hoots were like a lullaby to his weary ears.

'What's that noise?' Clive said. 'A sugar-bun buffalo?'

'It's Sammy snoring,' Cami giggled.

'And what's *that* noise?' Lucky asked.

Everyone stopped and listened to the peculiar flurry of snuffling and snorting. Louis shone his torch around the room. The light fell on Micky the mini-pig, who was laughing like a tickled pickle.

'Are you okay?' Lucky asked.

'Yes . . . I . . . It's . . . ' Micky gave another happy snort. 'This is the most fun I've had in my entire life!'

'Me too!' said Louis.

'Let's check out what else there is to see with our magic torches!' said Lucky.

'Yes! Let's go on a walk!' said Sammy, who had already woken up after his cat nap.

'It's *supposed* to be a sleepover,' said Clive with an exaggerated yawn. 'It must be past eight o'clock now and I need my beauty sleep.'

'We'll go to bed soon, Clive,' said Lucky with a smile. 'But we're all a bit excited to sleep right now! We need a little sleep walk.'

'NO,' Clive yapped. 'Mucky won't allow it. Will you, Mucky?'

'I certainly will,' Micky said. 'And the name is MICKY. Micky the Pickle! Er, I mean, pig.'

CHAPTER 7

Dark Night, Bright Idea

The cutes tiptoed through the museum with their torches, watching displays come to life. It was truly magical. Even Olive the night-shift security owl was having fun, swooping among the displays and hooting happily.

'This is amazing,' Lucky said.

'If you think that's amazing, look up!' said Sammy.

They were now in the Bones Room, where skeletons dangled from the ceiling. It was surely the creepiest hall in the museum. The friends pointed their torches upwards, nervous at the thought of giant monsters coming to life . . .

'WOW!' they all cried.

The eerie skeleton of a colossal squid had a surprisingly friendly face. And the giant teeth in a dinosaur head became the enormous friendly smile of a lesser-spotted grinosaurus.

They weren't scary at all!

'I never realised there was so much life in a museum,' Cami said, spinning around in the air among the skeletons.

'Everyone, listen up! I have the best idea,' Lucky said and the cutes gathered round. 'We're having fun because we've brought life back to the museum. If we can bring life back, then we can bring visitors back, too. These torches are the key! If people could see the museum come to life, it would change EVERYTHING.'

'It'll be a Museum of Interesting Excite-'ems!' Pip said with a giggle.

Dee chuckled. 'Instead of a museum, it'll be a NEW SEE 'UM!'

'Do you really think visitors will want to come if we give them torches?' Micky said.

'I've got another idea,' said Cami. 'I can see so many things that you can't, because they're out of reach. We have to bring everything closer.' She rained down little replicas of green squids and grinosauruses. The miniatures swam in front of the cutes' eyes, before popping into little green sparkles.

'YES!' yapped Louis. 'How can we help everyone to see things closer up?'

'I know!' said Lucky. She flapped her wings and flew up to join Cami. 'Let's make viewing platforms. Change everything around. Let's get this museum *off the ground*!'

There was a sharp little yap. Clive had something to say. Of course he did.

'As a descendant of the founder of the museum, I give my permission,' he barked. 'On one condition. The museum hangs a portrait of *me* on the wall.'

'I can draw the portrait right now?' Louis suggested.

'Brilliant idea, Louis,' Sammy said with a smile. It meant they could get on with things while Clive was posing for his picture.

The super cutes huddled together and discussed how to build new viewing platforms and bring the Museum of Most Important Items to life.

'It's a big job,' said Micky with a sigh. 'It'll take us all night.'

'Not with these it won't!' Dee said, sticking her paws deep in her pockets. She pulled out boxes of nails and screws, wood saws and an electric drill. 'They don't call me Dee the handicat for nothing.'

'*Do* they call you Dee the handi-cat?' Cami asked.

'No,' said Dee. 'But now's a good time to start.'

Micky opened up the storeroom, where they found all sorts of materials – planks, old doors, boxes and stepladders. Using Dee's incredible instant crafting skills, they built a huge helter-skelter so visitors would be able to climb right up to the ceiling beside the hanging exhibits and slide all the way down again, past the displays on the walls. Then they built a cart train out of boxes, to take kids on a journey through the museum. Old inflatable spacehoppers were taken from the toy display so visitors could bounce up to see the pictures on the walls. There were swinging seats and see-saws and zip wires. Louis the doodling labradoodle decorated all the new features and drew information displays.

Finally, the hard-working cutes stood still and admired what they'd created.

'Drab, drab, drab!' Clive yipped in disgust. 'If I'm to have anything to do with this museum, it just has to be fabulous!'

The chihuahua waved his little magic torch in the air. Instead of highlighting a disaster, it set everything in motion. Everything came to life! The helter-skelter flashed all colours. In the paintings on the walls, grasses swayed,

birds flapped and a sweet breeze drifted from the trees. Even the poo display woke up. The little lumps and swirls danced around and sorted themselves in order of colours of the rainbow.

'Who's the stinkiest of you lot?' Louis asked the poops.

The rainbow-coloured poop of the humpygrump hummingbird leaped up and spun around.

'You were right, Sammy!' Louis said with a laugh.

'Do you know what we've made?' Sammy said. 'We've made the Museum of the Magic and Marvellous.'

'The Magic and Marvellous!' they all whispered.

Micky snorted with glee. 'It's really old and totally brand new all at the same time!'

'We must do something to celebrate,' announced Clive, sashaying to the front.

The cutes were feeling a bit tired. But it was so rare that Clive thought about anyone but himself, they waited expectantly for his idea.

'As a treat,' Clive yapped, 'I'm going to give you a talk on my pedigree lineage. So, Clawdius Yapperton sailed the Popsicle Seas in search of artefacts for his collections, many of which are now in this museum. And his son, who went by the name of Barkit Furdiville –'

'SHHH!' said Micky firmly.

Clive's face puckered like an old rubber glove.

'It's Sammy's sleepover and Sammy makes the decisions,' said Micky.

Clive gulped and quivered. He was not used to being put in his place and he didn't know what to do. He pretended he had a sore paw and licked it. Sammy patted him on the head, which made his eyes blink.

'Thank you, Clive,' said Sammy kindly. 'Your talk would certainly make us sleepy. But before we go to bed, I have one more surprise.'

'Is it something to do with poo?' Pip asked.

'Not this time!' Sammy said with a laugh. 'How about a late-night treasure hunt?'

The cutes clapped with glee.

Cami cheered. 'A treasure hunt in a museum! What could be more fun?' she said. 'Sorry about your talk, Clive.'

Clive sniffed. 'That's fine with me, because I'll win the treasure hunt,' he said, stroking his tutu. 'I always win everything.'

'Not always,' muttered Pip. Everyone remembered Clive's awful singing at the Cuteness Competition.

'I've found a good hiding place,' Sammy said. 'I just need Louis to write and place the clues.'

'At your service,' Louis said, tapping his nose.

'And Micky is donating something from the giftshop as a prize!' Sammy added.

'What is it, Mucky?' demanded Clive. 'Tell me or I'll varnish your trotters an ugly shade of green.'

Micky ignored the silly chihuahua and trotted off to get the prize.

'Close your eyes until we're ready,' Sammy said. 'No peeking.'

Everyone waited with their eyes closed until Sammy, Micky and Louis returned to the main hall. Everyone except Clive, who said it was his ancestral right to keep an eye on anything that went on at the museum.

'Each clue is a picture of something in the museum *near* to where the next clue can be found!' Louis explained. 'Got it?' He handed the first clue to Dee.

'Then ready, steady, hunt!' Sammy called.

And as his friends rushed off to find a display of ancient clothes pegs, the sleepy sloth crawled inside the helter-skelter for a little snooze.

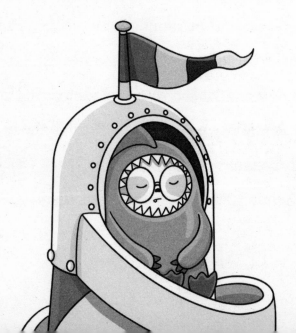

CHAPTER 7

The Quest for Rest

The friends skipped through the museum with Louis and Micky following behind. There were shrieks of delight as the magic torches lit up ancient items of beauty, like a dancing feather crown that once belonged to the Royal Peacock, and the Frozen Fountain of Angelica Falls, which sprayed jellied-fruit holograms. They pored over the clues together, and all of them worked as a team.

Well, not *all* of them.

Clive was on his own. If he worked out the treasure hunt with the others, how could he possibly win? He decided to forget the clues and look for the prize instead. He ran through the halls and rooms, yapping to put the cutes off, skidding across the slippery floors on his tiny nail-varnished paws.

The cutes let the chihuahua get on with it. At least while he was busy, they could enjoy the clue-finding.

'It's a picture of a sofa!' Lucky said, examining the latest clue. 'I know! Over there!'

They ran towards the ancient furniture

section, to a slouch couch that took you in its arms. Coming to life in the light of the magic torches, it grabbed Dee for a cuddle.

'This is *soooo* comfortable,' Dee mewed. 'I'll stay here while you look for the next clue.'

The others hunted around the slouch couch. Lucky grabbed a piece of paper from a water jug which swam with moving images of dolphins in the magic torchlight.

'Let me see, let me see!' Clive said, barging through with a slushie he'd stolen from the refreshments machine.

'But you haven't helped with any of the other clues,' Pip said.

Clive was furious. 'If I can't have it, neither

can *you*!' he yipped. And he tipped his slushie over the final clue.

In a flash Cami blew a freezing wind. It froze the slushie solid, so it fell and smashed on the floor. Clive shook with fury, prickling everyone yet again with his cactus spikes before storming off.

'Thanks, Cami,' Lucky said, grabbing the piece of paper. 'It's the final clue! A rhyming riddle.'

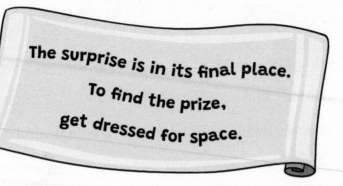

The surprise is in its final place.
To find the prize,
get dressed for space.

'Get dressed for space,' Dee murmured. 'What would I wear if I was going into space? A scarf, or maybe space socks?'

Lucky's eyes lit up. 'I saw a spacesuit in the costume section when we were building the swinging seats!'

'GO!' Cami, Dee, Pip, Louis, Olive and Micky all cheered. Sammy cheered too, crawling out of the helter-skelter to join the hunt – hoping no one had noticed his little snooze.

Lucky half ran, half flew down a corridor

and into a large hall with her friends close behind. Through the high windows, the moon covered the floor with ribbons of light. Everyone sighed with happiness as Lucky's magic horn began to glow.

'We'll never get bored of your incredible lunar-horn, Lucky!' Pip cheered.

Lucky lit up the displays with her magic horn. Wow! The ice-cream maker's uniform sparkled with sprinkles, the silk layers on the Fairy Queen's dress floated all on their own . . . and there was the spacesuit! The reflection of stars moved across the visor and its padded arms floated in the air.

Lucky quickly wriggled into the costume.

Her head slotted into the helmet, her horn still glowing in the moonlight. Then the magic in her torch made the spacesuit float. She was suspended in mid-air, glowing and beaming with happiness.

'Hooray for Lucky the space lunacorn!' Dee shouted.

'What a great prize!' said Cami.

'That's not the prize,' Micky said. 'Search your space pockets, Lucky!'

Lucky pulled something out of a pocket and held it up. A plastic star.

'Lovely,' she said, trying to sound enthusiastic. 'Thanks, Micky.'

The mini-pig sighed. 'I know it's not much. The gift shop's a bit rubbish, really.'

'Why don't we shine magic on it?' Sammy suggested. He pointed his torch at Lucky's star.

The star shook as if it was filling with energy. Then, suddenly, it shot up into the air, spinning and dancing, zooming across the ceiling, trailing tiny glittering stars in its wake like a firework.

'WHOA!' everyone gasped.

'Star, stop!' Lucky said. The star shot straight back into her space pocket. 'A very obedient shooting star,' she said, laughing. 'That's the best prize *ever.*'

'It's MINE!' came a sharp little bark. 'MINE!'

Clive had slipped in to the back of the hall and seen the whole thing. His nose twitched and his lips curled back, revealing pointy little teeth. A growl rolled in the back of his throat.

'Lunacorns can't use spacesuits,' he barked furiously. 'Not allowed. Only dogs have been in space. Me, I'm a dog. It's MY prize.'

Sammy shrugged apologetically. 'Actually,

there have been many animals in space – cats, monkeys, rabbits, jellyfish . . . And one day, there'll be a lunacorn, too.'

'It's a stitch-up!' the chihuahua shouted. 'I demand another hunt! ARRRGHGHGH!'

Clive ran around the room like an out-of-control bicycle, before collapsing in the middle of the floor on his tummy. He rolled around and banged his little paws in a proper tantrum. The spines from his cactus came off and his tutu was ripped to shreds.

Sammy put his arm around the weeping chihuahua. 'I think you're just very tired, Clive,' he said. 'Let's curl up and tell some stories before we get some sleep.'

'Great idea, Sammy,' Cami said. She yawned and rained little pillows.

'Perhaps this will help,' said Dee, and produced insta-choc blocks from her pockets.

MMMMM!

Back in the sleepover room, snuggled in their sleeping bags, the super cutes cradled mugs of hot choc and felt their eyes droop. Louis drew dreamy patterns on the tent canopy and Dee shone her magic torch on them so they moved like hypnotic whirlpools.

'This is so wonderful, Sammy,' Lucky said sleepily. 'Being here, in this magical place with my best friends . . . It's the best sleepover ever.'

'It really is,' Cami agreed.

'Have you had fun, Clive?' Sammy asked. He looked at the little dog and hoped to see a smile, or even just a little tail wag.

But Clive was too busy looking in a pocket mirror. Sammy felt a little bit sorry for him. The chihuahua would have so much more fun if he didn't think about himself all the time!

'How are you feeling, Pip?' Cami said, snuggling up.

'Fine,' Pip said with a sleepy smile. 'It's not so bad being away from home when you feel like you're with family.'

'That's lovely, Pip,' Lucky said, curling her legs under her body and folding her wings over Dee and Sammy for extra warmth.

Clive curled himself up in a tight chihuahua ball with his back to the group. He was soon fast asleep and making little snorey whistles. *He can be cute – sometimes!* Sammy thought.

'You've got lovely friends,' Micky whispered, snugging deep inside his sleeping bag.

Sammy smiled. 'And now you're one of them.'

Micky blinked happily, then yawned and closed his eyes.

CHAPTER 8

A Great ~~Escape~~ Success

The cutes slept soundly and didn't wake up until the morning, when a waft of breakfast pancakes tickled their nostrils. They sat up and stretched and grinned at each other. They'd just had the best sleepover party ever! They looked around at everything they'd created – the helter-skelter, the brilliant displays and the playgrounds of curiosity. Louis had made a sign, too. It was strung across the room.

Welcome to the Museum of the Magic and the Marvellous!

'It's a new day in our new museum,' Sammy said.

'Wakey, wakey!' Micky came out of the Museum Café, flipping a huge pancake in a frying pan. He was still dressed in his onesie  but with an apron around his middle. 'Breakfast is being served! And if you don't hurry, that little dog is going to eat *everything*.'

'My prize!' Lucky wailed suddenly. 'I put my shooting star right next to my pillow and now it's gone.'

'Oh dear,' Sammy said. 'I was hoping that our friendship might have changed Clive's ways.'

'Let's move on the quick double-flip!' Pip said. 'We'll catch him while he's eating breakfast.'

They ran to the café – but Clive had gone. There was mess everywhere. The selfish little dog had helped himself to all the toppings – maple syrup, strawberry slices, banana chunks, and blueberries . . . And there was a purple trail of squished-blueberry pawprints leading to the door.

'Follow those pawprints!' Cami called.

They ran after Clive. He was only a little dog with very little legs. If they were quick, they would catch him –

'**OW!** My leg!' Lucky cried. She had tripped over something, but what? There was nothing there!

'That's strange,' said Sammy with a frown. 'Come on, let's hurry.'

They entered a library stacked with old dusty books. Clive's purple footprints crossed the tiles to a door on the far side.

'OW!' This time it was Pip who fell over. 'I just tripped up, too! And I wasn't being clumsy!'

Cami touched a little wire strung across the doorway. It snapped back. 'Elastic tripwires!' she gasped.

Sammy tutted. 'What a rascal!'

Cami led the way, flicking the tripwires so they disappeared and the others could hurry through each doorway without any trouble.

Then the trail of the blueberry footsteps stopped.

They were in a greenhouse, filled with ancient trees. There was no other way out. So Clive had to be hiding here – somewhere . . .

'A giraffe tree!' Pip cried. She pointed to a floppy tree with a brown spotty trunk.

'And a pom-pom tree!' said Dee in excitement. When she patted the pom-pom tufts, they shrank away from her paws and then puffed out again.

'And a chihuahua tree!' Lucky said.

With the shooting star clamped firmly in his teeth, Clive had scaled an enormous palm tree and was close to the glass roof. A small skylight was open. The cheeky chihuahua was sneaking out of the museum with the stolen star!

'Stop!' Sammy called.

'My forefather is Clawdius Yapperton!' Clive snarled around the prize in his mouth. 'By rights this star is mine!'

Micky undid his apron and fixed his museum hat firmly on his head. 'Let's get him! Lucky?'

Lucky nodded. 'Hop on, Micky.'

'We're coming too!' said Sammy and Cami.

Dee was still distracted by the pom-pom tree, but Micky jumped on Lucky's back and Sammy held on to Cami. The four cutes flew to the very top of the greenhouse and looked down at Clive.

He was balancing precariously on the top of the palm tree.

'Cami, what do you think we should do with Clive?' Lucky asked.

'I think we should make him wet,' said Cami.

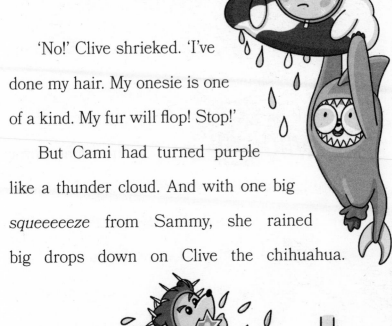

'No!' Clive shrieked. 'I've done my hair. My onesie is one of a kind. My fur will flop! Stop!'

But Cami had turned purple like a thunder cloud. And with one big *squeeeeeze* from Sammy, she rained big drops down on Clive the chihuahua.

Clive scrambled to cover his head. As he did so, the prize slipped from his teeth and tumbled towards the ground.

WHOOSH! Silent as the night, Olive the night-shift security owl swooped through the greenhouse and plucked the star from the air, placing it safely on Lucky's back.

'Thank you, Olive!' Lucky cried. 'You came just in time!'

But they were too late to stop Clive escaping. In the commotion, he had leaped from the palm tree and grabbed the window frame. Now he was wriggling through the skylight, out into the open. He stared down at the cutes through the glass, bedraggled and furious. Then he slid all the way down the roof on his cactus bottom.

'What's he doing?' Pip gasped.

'That's dangerous!' Cami cried. 'He'll hurt himself.'

The super cutes rushed to the greenhouse windows. They got there in time to see Clive land on a large inflatable beach ball. He bounced to his feet, hopped on a scooter and zoomed away.

'The Glamour Gang!' cried the cutes.

Lucky spotted all the members of the Glamour Gang – the scooter, the pizza slice, the snail and the angry muffin. The Glamour Gang followed Clive everywhere. They must have been waiting outside for him all night!

Micky banged on the window furiously.

Clive turned round with a victorious grin.

'The museum has a new name, so your lifetime membership doesn't count!' Micky shouted. 'And you're BANNED!' He looked at his watch and squeaked. 'Ooh! It's nearly opening time!'

Forget Clive – there was too much to do!

The cutes rolled up the sleeping bags, straightened the plants, washed up in the café and cleaned everything left over from the fun of the night before. When everything was in place, they shone their magic torches to make sure everything was working. The helter-skelter lit up with neon lights and the wagon-train trundled through the halls. The displays moved and waved and then . . . the fossils arrived.

'Are you sure about this?' Sammy asked. 'The fossils are a museum treasure!'

'What's the point in keeping them hidden away?' said Micky as the fossils zoomed about. He straightened the brand-new uniform that Dee had made specially for him. It was red and white with the museum's new name embroidered on the back in sparkle thread. He'd even cleaned his wellies. 'I just hope that people will come and see them.'

Lucky peeked through the keyhole in the giant doors.

'I don't think your museum will be shutting down any time soon,' she said.

The night before, the light from the super cutes' magic torches had created a dazzling light show in the skies above the museum. Now every cute in Marshmallow Canyon and beyond wanted to see what it was all about. The queue wrapped round the block!

'Is there anyone out there?' Micky asked nervously.

Lucky smiled. 'Just a few,' she said. 'We're going to stick around all day to help you, too.'

Micky reached out a trotter and patted every single one of his new friends. 'Thank you. Thanks to ALL of you.'

The smart little pig took a big breath, ready for his BIG moment. He swung open the doors and stepped out in front of the huge crowd. He looked back at his friends, shocked.

'*Just a few*?' he said. 'There are hundreds!' And his cheeks blushed with happiness.

The super cute friends smiled at each other. They'd done it! They'd turned the stuffy old museum into an exciting place to explore the magical history of the World of Cute. And they'd done it together.

'Three cheers for the museum!' Lucky said. 'Hip, hip, hooray! Hip, hip, hooray! Hip, hip . . . OH!'

With a giant **POP** that made the whole crowd jump, Lucky's luna-horn exploded with confetti, glitter and candies. The sparkling shower fell in slow motion through the crowd, who whooped and whistled and clapped, chanting, 'Let us in! Let us in!'

With another twitch of Lucky's horn and another great POP! all the lights inside the museum streamed through the windows in

lots of different colours, forming a giant rainbow ribbon that arced over the museum.

'I didn't know it would do that!' Lucky gasped.

'What a grand opening celebration!' Micky said. He faced the crowd and boomed in his biggest voice: 'I DECLARE THE MUSEUM OF THE MAGIC AND MARVELLOUS . . . OPEN!'

'And I declare that I've just had the best sleepover party of my life,' Sammy said, looking at his amazing super cute friends. 'I'll admit, there were a couple of prickly moments and lots of surprises . . . but it was perfect.'

The super cutes laughed. And away in the distance, the Wish Tree rustled happily, ready to grant its next wonderful wish.

More magical fun in the world of Super Cute, out now!

CHAPTER ONE

We're Glowing to Charm Glade!

Lucky the lunacorn had an invitation in her bag to a *very* special occasion. It was taking place on the other side of Charm Glade and she had been flying all night to get there! But when sunrise came, Lucky just had to stop. The World of Cute was waking up and it was an amazing thing to watch.

Lucky landed in the Dipsy Daisy Meadow and gazed happily as the golden beams tickled the multi-coloured grasses. Flowers lifted their sleepy heads, little creatures emerged from their dens and birds rose from the treetops, swooping and singing. The start of a new day was always enchanting. But today, as distant music drifted on the breeze, Lucky sensed something especially magical in the air.

'I must be close to Charm Glade!' she said to herself.

'I must be close to Charm Glade!' repeated a chorus of voices.

Lucky felt a bit confused. Then she spotted long ears and cotton tails in the grass around her. 'Oh, it's the funny bunnies!' she said.

'Funny bunnies!' the bunnies giggled, springing one by one from the undergrowth like popcorn. They stopped in mid-air to do star jumps and cartwheels, before tumbling back down again. Lucky watched in awe.

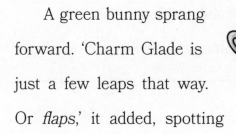

A green bunny sprang forward. 'Charm Glade is just a few leaps that way. Or *flaps*,' it added, spotting Lucky's wings. It looked down at Lucky's hooves. 'Or gallops . . . What kind of creature *are* you?'

3

'A lunacorn,' Lucky replied.

'A lunacorn,' gasped the bunnies. 'Wow!'

'I'm like a unicorn, but with a very special horn,' Lucky explained.

The bunnies stared in confusion at the normal-looking horn on the top of Lucky's head.

'It's not doing anything now,' said Lucky. 'But when the moon comes out, it *glows*!'

'**WOW!**' said the bunnies again.

Lucky had always known that one day her horn would glow and be ready to perform magic. She had waited so long for it to happen, she worried it never would! But that very night, as the moon rose high, her horn had dazzled for the very first time. Lucky had been so excited,

4

she'd swooped through the air, twisting and turning like an acrobatic star. Her glowing horn was now guiding her through the marshmallow canyons toward Charm Glade.

Now that her horn had started to glow, it meant the magic was brewing. And surely it wouldn't be long before Lucky discovered what that magic would be . . .

'It will happen when the time is right,' her mum had said.

Lucky hoped the right time would happen soon. And she REALLY hoped her horn would do something super cool!

'Are you going to the Blossom Festival?' asked an orange bunny.

Lucky nodded. 'And this year I'm entering the Cuteness Competition.'

'You *are* quite cute,' said a white bunny, ears turning pink as she blushed.

'Thank you very much,' said Lucky. 'So are you! But the Cuteness Competition is not about what you look like. It's a contest to show everyone what makes you special.'

'And what makes *you* special?' the white-and-pink bunny asked.

'My horn, of course!' Lucky laughed. 'I must be on my way now. Nice to meet you all. Bye!'

The bunnies tumbled like bouncy balls back into the grasses and Lucky took off into the sky, to continue her journey among the candyfloss clouds.

As the sun rose higher, the World of Cute burst into colour. Candy blossoms popped open in the heat. Lucky was flying above a Smiley Sunflower Field when she saw an irresistible sight – a crystal-clear pond.

'Surely another quick stop won't hurt,' she said to herself.

She landed and dipped her head to drink. The water was sweet and cold, instantly washing away her tiredness.

I'm refreshed and ready for the competition! Lucky thought. Now to check the details . . .

Lucky pulled the slip of paper from the

backpack and was opening her invitation when, all of a sudden, strange noises erupted behind her. Rustles, snuffles and whistles. They seemed to be coming from a single sunflower – a sunflower with its petals still closed. Lucky crept closer and saw a tiny snoring sushi-mouse cradled inside.

'Hello, little –' she began.

'SHHH. Don't wake Dylan! He's v-e-r-y grumpy in the mornings!'

The owner of the voice sprang from nowhere and landed at Lucky's feet. Actually it landed ON Lucky's feet. She squeaked in surprise and dropped her invitation. It was . . . a pineapple! And it was wearing goggles!